NOVEL TITLES
BY RENEE GOODWIN

A Love, A Life Forgone

GG LIFE LESSON STORYBOOK SERIES ®
BY RENEE GOODWIN

GG Cleans House – Learning Teamwork
GG Meets Her Match – Becoming Forever Friends
GG Asks, "Is Jesus In Your Class?" – Seek, Know, Guide, Inspire
GG Takes Action – Practicing Health Safety

Living Past Shadows

Living Past Shadows

Renee Goodwin

GGP

Goodwin Global
Publishing

GOODWIN GLOBAL PUBLISHING, LLC
TYLER, TEXAS

Copyright © 2022 by Renee Goodwin
All rights reserved.
First Edition

Goodwin Global Publishing, LLC
Tyler, TX

Published by Goodwin Global Publishing, LLC 2022

ISBN 979-8-9869964-5-5 (paperback)
ISBN 979-8-9869964-6-2 (digital)

Book layout and design by Gabriela Fleming
Cover design by Renee Goodwin and Gabriela Fleming
Author photograph by Diana Cassetta-Perez

Printed in the United States of America

DEDICATION

For all living past shadows to new beginnings.

Living Past Shadows

TABLE OF CONTENTS

PART I

CHAPTER 1

Jodie

My adrenaline was flowing. My mind was in a stir. I had been driving for hours. All I could remember was filling Roy to the brim and continuing onward. Foregoing a very needed pit stop, afraid to deter one minute, I fought fatigue and exhaustion in my quest seeking safety as fast as I could. I left Kansas in a rush, traveled through Oklahoma and was making my way deep into Texas. Hours of driving later, still in Texas, I confirmed what I had heard people say, "Texas is a Big State." Roy, my beloved truck and I forged ahead praying to find a safe haven.

Roy gifted me with 100,000 memorable miles. Roy didn't ask for much, a little oil here, a new tire there and Roy was back on the road again. Right now, I did not want to remember one mile much less 100,000 miles of my past journeys. I knew running was not the answer but honestly, I did not care. I was only interested in how fast and how far I could travel away from the miseries I left behind. I know I can never remove the hurt from my heart. My heart is pierced for life. But I want to stop living past shadows, shadows of tragedies and sorrows and start living past shadows opening doors for a new future.

Pedal to the metal not looking in my rearview mirror I raced on.

CHAPTER 2

Roy

I was startled as Jodie jumped into my cab, put the gearshift in drive, accelerator pedal to the floor and we raced down the road. Jodie never looked back. I was not sure where we were going but I was glad we were going.

CHAPTER 3

Jodie

The sky was growing dark as the red-orange sun glowed easing below the horizon. The temperature was cooling making driving conditions tolerable. I was guessing it must have been a 90-degree day. Yet riding in Roy it felt closer to 100 degrees. Poor Roy's air conditioning faltered around the 75,000-mile mark but I didn't have the money needed to fix the system. Definitely, the air conditioning was not the only item needing work. I hoped one day for a smoother ride and a better look would come our way once I could afford new shocks and a paint job. For now, I trust Roy will stay road worthy and we can get to a safe place.

CHAPTER 4

Roy

With Jodie's below par driving, I could tell she did not have her mind on the road. I know she must be very tired and very hot. I could tell my radiator was at its max temperature. We had been on the road for hours with the hours adding up becoming days.

I did my best to keep my headlights shining ahead making a clear and safe path hoping we would find a hideaway soon.

CHAPTER 5

Jodie

Wiping the sweat from my brow I took a moment to embrace the surroundings. There were children playing in the park across the street. It seemed they were trying to get one last merry-go-round ride before calling it a day. Looking down the town's main street, the local vendors were turning out the store lights. I noticed the shop owners did not bother to lock the doors. Some got in their cars and drove away. Others strolled down the sidewalk to the diner on the corner. I recalled the sign I read entering the town, "Honest, Texas, 2019 Population 254, Everyone Welcome!" At this point in my life, I pray that is an honest statement.

Seeing the diner down the street, now thinking of food, my stomach began to grumble. I tried to remember when and where I ate last. Recalling it actually was not a meal at all, a soft drink and chips during a pit stop a while ago. Searching my pockets, I scraped together $6.56. Opening the diner door the nightly special sign advertised, chicken-fried chicken, mashed potatoes and gravy, $5.99. I felt sad I would not be able to leave much of a tip but my mouth was watering just at the thought of a hot, tasty meal.

I took a seat near the window toward the rear of the diner. The waitress welcomed me with a huge smile and a Texas twang accent. "Howdy, welcome to Honest. I hope you are hungry. We are serving up a great special tonight, chicken, taters and gravy. If you have room afterwards, I recommend our pecan pie for dessert." I shyly replied, "I will have the special, that's all." Moments later I was served a plate of hot, steamy fried chicken overflowing with potatoes and gravy dripping down the sides. I gave the waitress a quick thank you as I grabbed my knife and fork scooping the first bite.

The smell of the fried food, the salty taste of the potatoes took me back to the summer days spent with my grandparents years ago. Those were such happy days I love to remember. Suddenly, the memory of the last moments with NaNa and PaPa streamed through my mind. I started to choke. Everyone in the diner looked my way. I grabbed the receipt, left my $6.56 on the table and walked out as fast as I could.

Trying to clear my throat and mind, I looked up and down the street for lodging. I had a few dollars tucked away in my bag I had saved from working at the library, which seemed forever ago now. A few blocks away there was a neon motel sign blinking, "Vacancy." I hopped into the cab and headed Roy toward what I hoped would be a good night's sleep. The motel manager was pleasant enough, giving me the key to #108, pointed me in the direction to the room and wished me a good night. After a lukewarm shower, I towel dried my hair, dressed in the only set of clothes I was able to grab in my rush to leave, then collapsed on the bed trying not to think about bedbugs.

* * *

I fell into a deep sleep dreaming of the summer of 2012 when I came to stay with NaNa and PaPa. I was a recent college graduate anxious to arrive at NaNa and PaPa's farm. Thinking of the landscape, beautiful, green rolling hills, as the backdrop for the huge red barn and country house, brought to mind the scent of coastal hay mixed with honeysuckle. During past summers when I visited NaNa and PaPa, I would watch the honeybees for hours sucking the sweet nectar from the flowers as they spread pollen from one bloom to another.

I studied ranch management in college and was excited to begin lending a helping hand on my grandparents' farm. Not having a vehicle, I took a taxi cab traveling a few miles from the county airport to the farm. The cab driver honked the horn and NaNa came running from the house and PaPa quickened his step skipping from the barn along with the devoted farm animals. Silo, the black and white tomcat was always happy to share his trophy catches, usually field mice. Duke, the amazing Border collie mix made the task herding the cattle a cinch. Duke enjoyed herding people just the same. He was not particular. Then, there was Hercules whinnying from his stall, a beautiful black stallion when in his prime could outrun the best Kentucky Derby contenders. It was truly a blessing for all, especially Silo, Duke and Hercules that they found their way to the farm to spend their retirement years.

With the animals jumping up and down, the hugging began. NaNa and PaPa always gave me hugs that lasted forever it seemed. As I hugged NaNa, I smelled the scent of fresh baked bread. Of course, PaPa reeked of diesel fuel. PaPa spent many a waking hour on the farm tractors, cutting, baling, and then stacking hay bundles. Living on the farm meant working hard day in and day out but, NaNa and PaPa really knew no other life.

Slowly everyone moved toward the house. As I suspected there were two loaves of fresh homemade bread cooling on the rack. I didn't know if I could wait until morning to taste NaNa's mouthwatering bread slathered with homemade berry jam. NaNa saw the look in my eyes and said, "Let's all have a slice of bread and jam." NaNa added, "I have a chocolate pie in the icebox for after supper." My eyes grew even larger. Oh, chocolate anything was my favorite. From years of taste testing, I knew NaNa's pies were as delicious as her breads and jams.

As we finished our snack, PaPa suggested that I come to the barn to see some equipment he acquired from a neighbor. I loved touring the barn. There was always something to see I had not noticed before. As PaPa was bragging on his new hay baler, I noticed a picture hanging on the wall above PaPa's tool bench of me with my parents. I immediately recognized the setting. It was the 1998 Kay County Harvest Fest. When I was 8 years old, my parents took me to the Fest for the first time and then every year after that until I went to college.

* * *

Holding the picture, I closed my eyes remembering the great times I shared with Mom and Dad at the Fest. First things first, we headed to the food area. We ate hotdogs loaded with cheese and chili, corn-on-the-cob-on-a-stick dripping with margarine, and funnel cakes sprinkled with powdered sugar. Then, we happily washed it all down with a homemade lemonade. No matter what tactics I tried, my mouth stayed covered with powdered sugar from the funnel cake sticking to the margarine rimming my lips from the corn-on-the-cob.

Now all fed, Mom, Dad and I strolled over to the rides. Year after year I, and especially my stomach questioned why we ate first then rode the rides instead of in the reverse order. I thought, "Oh well, queasy stomach and all, the fest was tons of fun." My dad favored riding the Tilt-A-Whirl. He would spin us round and round as we belly laughed. My mom enjoyed riding the Ferris Wheel. My mom and I would ride over and over again throughout the day. We particularly enjoyed our sunset ride. We loved when the ride stopped at the very top.

Oh, the view was magnificent. We could see the vast pastureland, the rolling green hills and the golden sun setting on the horizon.

* * *

I heard PaPa call my name as I replaced the picture on the wall. Papa summoned me to look at his new tractor hay rake. It was an impressive piece of machinery, but I was more interested in a vehicle bumper I spied peeking out from underneath a dusty tarp. I walked over to the tarp to get a closer look, fighting endless cobwebs along the way. Fearing rats, snakes and surely more cobwebs, I slowly pulled back the tarp uncovering a pickup truck that had definitely seen better days.

I was mesmerized. I wondered why I had never noticed this great surprise before. Bubbling with excitement, I called to PaPa, "Look what I found. Where did this truck come from? How long has it been here? Does it run?" PaPa waving his hands, tried to slow my questions. "Just a minute, let me catch up." PaPa explained he surprised NaNa with the truck when they first moved to the country. NaNa was expecting and he wanted to make sure they would be able to get to the hospital for the baby's birth.

CHAPTER 6

Roy

Remembering

It was a surprise, alright. NaNa was getting into my cab as fast as she could waddle. PaPa was over the top excited, he was not thinking straight. He threw a suitcase in the back so hard I got an everlasting dent. Then, PaPa took off in the wrong direction. I had to overtake the steering and get him back on track. I went as fast and as safely as I could. NaNa was in great pain. She tried not to scream but with every breath she could manage, a shrill was exhaled.

Pulling up to the hospital emergency entrance, the hospital staff hurried out to help NaNa into a wheelchair. PaPa followed everyone into the hospital and forgot to take me to the parking lot. I was worried for NaNa and the baby and I was worried I would get towed and not be near to help if needed.

After a while, PaPa remembered to come back to me. He jumped in with a huge smile on his face saying, "Roy, it is a boy, a beautiful, handsome boy. Roy, thank you for helping us get to the hospital, helping keep all of us safe. Roy, I can always trust in you."

Oh, my battery overflowed with pride.

CHAPTER 7

Jodie

I slowly opened my eyes to unfamiliar surroundings. Startled, I jumped out of bed, ran and opened the door. There was Roy, my everlasting trusty truck. Thank goodness. Seeing Roy helped my nerves calm and my mind begin to clear. Then, thoughts of the happenings from the previous days and nights quickly returned.

Taking a few breaths, I sat at the foot of the bed contemplating my options. I did not want to run from one nightmare then create another. No matter how rotten Randy was or was becoming, I knew with NaNa and PaPa near me, I would be safe from his harm. But, since NaNa and PaPa's passing, I felt vulnerable to Randy's vices. I no longer had protection.

I needed a plan to find a safe place. But, having little money, my choices were very limited. However, somehow, step by step I was determined to go forward with my life.

But right now, I am so tired I cannot think clearly. I need more rest.

Oh, I wish Mom and Dad, NaNa and PaPa were still with me.

CHAPTER 8

Roy

I was relieved seeing Jodie quickly poke her head out of the motel room door. It had been several days since I saw her. I knew she was tired. I was exhausted. Getting a little rest was good for both of us.

Jodie closed the door! When is she coming out again? I really think for her safety, we must keep moving. We need permanent shelter and safety. Should I sound my horn to get her attention? Yet, I am still so tired, I don't think I have battery power for even a small horn toot.

CHAPTER 9

Jodie

Remembering

I came to visit PaPa and NaNa one day. They immediately sensed something was wrong. I was not my chipper self. It was hard to hide my red and swollen eyes. NaNa asked me, "Sweetheart, are you coming down with a cold? It is getting to be that time of year." I answered as cheerfully as I could, "No, NaNa. I am feeling alright. Just a little tired I suppose." PaPa and NaNa knew my tiredness was really sadness. But they did not want to pry.

When I stayed for only a short while, PaPa and NaNa were sure something was troubling me. They guessed, most probably, my troubles centered around Randy. PaPa and NaNa were always cordial to Randy. They definitely wanted me to be happy. As a married couple, PaPa and NaNa knew marriage has its difficult moments. PaPa and NaNa always promised each other not to hold in ill feelings. They promised to talk through their differences knowing their marriage would be stronger and happier in the end.

With Randy away with the rodeo months at a time, PaPa and NaNa knew days of separation can wear on a couple and their marriage. They were concerned my five years of wedding bliss with Randy were no longer. NaNa and PaPa suspected something had changed as they witnessed me trying my best to hide my broken heart.

Since the tragic loss of my parents, my beloved Mom and Dad, known to all as Brad and Dorothy, I was PaPa and NaNa's forever love. I knew on earth or in spirit PaPa and NaNa would always be watching over me.

CHAPTER 10

Roy

I remember the day Jodie and I went to visit PaPa and NaNa. Jodie was trying her best to hide what I call her "Randy Disappointments." PaPa and NaNa were not fooled. While NaNa occupied Jodie baking and canning, PaPa drove me to town. PaPa told me he was going to visit their family attorney, Thomas Riley. I sensed PaPa's trip must be very important.

Sure enough. About an hour later, PaPa returned with a handful of papers. He reviewed the papers speaking out loud, "Roy, when NaNa and I go see the Lord, Jodie will be well taken care of." PaPa put the papers in my glove box for the moment intending to place them in a safe place at home.

CHAPTER 11

Jodie

NaNa and PaPa's earthly departure was so sudden. Remembering, I stopped by to visit NaNa and PaPa. I started helping NaNa bake bread and can jams and jellies. PaPa visited for a while then asked to borrow Roy. PaPa said he had an errand to run, he was going into town and would be back shortly.

As NaNa bent down, peeking into the oven checking the bread, she collapsed. I went to help her up but she was unresponsive. At that moment I heard Roy's familiar engine humming up the drive. I ran to get PaPa's help. Within minutes, I was behind the wheel, PaPa was holding NaNa, and Roy raced us to the hospital.

Roy

Pulling up to the house, Jodie came running out screaming, "PaPa, NaNa collapsed. Hurry, hurry!!!" Within minutes, PaPa and Jodie had NaNa in my cab and off I raced to the hospital. I had to help save NaNa.

Jodie

The doctors reported NaNa had slipped into a coma. She stayed hospitalized for several weeks, the specialists trying every treatment possible. Nothing seemed to work. Then, one night with PaPa and I at her bedside, holding her hands, NaNa took her last breath.

PaPa and I were devastated. As I watched the tears stream down PaPa's face, day after day, I felt totally overwhelmed and helpless. Randy saw me grieving but made no effort to console. I stayed with PaPa as much as I could but at the same time trying not to let my responsibilities lapse at my house. I did not waste my time thinking Randy may pitch in to help. Randy had proved time after time, it was all about Randy.

I did my best to hide my failing relationship with Randy from NaNa and PaPa. Now, especially I did not want to add to PaPa's grief. I was managing both households as best as I could. After a few months, PaPa was still in a state of shock with NaNa gone. He would not leave the house. He had not been working the farm or even been out to the barn. PaPa stayed in the kitchen trying to understand why NaNa had gone to heaven so early in her life and without him.

PaPa and I asked ourselves over and over again, "Why did NaNa have to die?" Not knowing the medical reasoning behind NaNa's passing made it even more difficult for PaPa and I to go forward. Did NaNa suffer from breathing complications? Was that the cause of her death? As a child, NaNa battled through a serious case of pneumonia leaving her lungs weak. Or did NaNa collapse from years of hard work living a life on the farm?

PaPa and I had many unanswered questions stirring within. We tried to find some level of peace and comfort, but time stood still for both of us. Then, the many questions never answered surrounding my parents' deaths that I had suppressed for years came flooding back into my mind again adding more grief.

CHAPTER 12

Jodie

I contained my emotions as best as I could. It was extremely difficult watching PaPa wilt away. PaPa kept telling me he had no reason to live without NaNa. NaNa was his life. PaPa and NaNa loved to tell the story of how they met and I enjoyed listening each time. Through the years, I kept their story close to my heart. PaPa told the story saying,

"The first time I saw her face, I knew she was the only girl for me. It was the summer of 1963. NaNa's given name was Nancy Wilson. Nancy (NaNa) and her family were visiting relatives in my hometown. I was known to my family and friends as George, although my given name was Paul Hall. Over the years I was teased having rhyming names. To skirt the issue, I told everyone my name was George.

NaNa and her friends strolled into the drugstore where I worked as a soda jerk. I kindly nudged my buddy Stan over to the side and made my way to take NaNa's order. She ordered her favorite treat; vanilla ice cream with chocolate syrup, a sprinkle of pecans but hold the cherry. As NaNa attempted to eat her dessert, I could tell she was distracted by my stares. I was staring, lost in her beautiful, bright blue eyes.

I mustered the courage needed and asked NaNa to the movie. *Beach Party* with Frankie Avalon and Annette

Funicello was playing that night at the Bijou Theater. My buddies told me NaNa was visiting from the East Coast so I thought she would feel at home watching a beach movie.

I had just enough money saved. A movie ticket for the early evening showing was $.65, a bag of popcorn was $.75 and $1.00 for a soda. I considered this money my special occasion money. My real money as I called it, I was saving to buy a truck I had my eyes on down at Stu's Auto Sales."

* * *

Born in 1944, PaPa had a meager existence, a shanty for a house, hand-me-downs for clothing and limited food to eat. PaPa worked for the neighbors, doing chores but got a job as soon as he was old enough at the gas station. He made $2.00 an hour working after school and on Saturdays. When he was not working at the gas station, he filled in at the drugstore soda fountain.

It was clear to see for NaNa, PaPa and everyone around, NaNa and PaPa were made for each other. They were inseparable. NaNa was an expert seamstress. She could sew dresses, tops, pants, shorts. You name it, NaNa could sew it without a pattern. In NaNa's hometown, she worked at the fabric store after school. The store manager let NaNa have the fabric remnants and since NaNa did not have a sewing machine, the store manager let NaNa use a sewing machine at the fabric store. After store hours, NaNa would stay and let her creations materialize. NaNa displayed some of her items in the windows of the fabric store. Window shoppers would comment on the quality and perfection of NaNa's work. Customers purchased

NaNa's items and the store manager let NaNa have the money. NaNa was saving her money to go to college to study home economics.

However, after meeting PaPa, NaNa's plans changed. PaPa and NaNa were married fall '63. They rented a small home at the edge of town. PaPa delayed buying the truck he wanted. Instead, PaPa bought NaNa a sewing machine as a wedding gift. The fabric store manager from NaNa's hometown would send her scraps of material and NaNa continued sewing her designs and selling garments from their home. PaPa began working full-time as the gas station manager. But PaPa and NaNa still made time to go to the soda fountain at the drugstore where they first met to share their favorite ice cream delight.

* * *

Expecting their first child (my dad) the next year, PaPa and NaNa moved to the country. They had saved enough money to purchase a few acres of land with a quaint little house and a barn. Needing transportation now that NaNa and PaPa lived outside of town, using the farm as collateral, PaPa secured a loan to buy the truck he so wanted. PaPa brought home their 1960 Ford F-100 truck. He bragged to NaNa showing off the 186-hp, 292-cu.in. V-8 engine under the hood. NaNa knew very little about vehicles but she smiled and played along. Sharing his excitement made her happy and proud. PaPa finished his sales pitch showing off the truck's sporty grille and parking lamps. NaNa liked the color. PaPa described the two-tone color as titanium white on the hood and cab and vermilion red on the sides. PaPa named the truck Roy.

* * *

The memories of those wonderful years PaPa shared with NaNa; those beautiful moments together were all he had left. But the memories were not enough. Shortly after NaNa's passing, one night PaPa went to bed to an eternal sleep. Seeing the peaceful expression on PaPa's face, I was comforted knowing he and NaNa were reunited for everlasting happiness.

Saying goodbye to NaNa and PaPa, I relived the time having to say goodbye to my parents all over again. I felt myself falling into that deep, dark place. Even more devastating was acknowledging the fact that I was now totally vulnerable to Randy's vices. Although my whole being was telling me I needed to allow myself to mourn and grieve, I knew I had to plan and act quickly to save myself.

CHAPTER 13

Roy

Ever since NaNa and PaPa's passing, Jodie has been petrified of Randy. Her body was filled with anguish. Her face darkened with fear. I was afraid Randy would really hurt her. Before, Randy knowing that NaNa and PaPa may stop by anytime, Randy never raised a hand to Jodie in his irate moments but he yelled and yelled and yelled. Parked out front in the yard, looking through the picture window, I could see Jodie standing strong, taking his verbal ranting and raving, cruel words she did not deserve.

* * *

I tried to give Jodie all the horsepower my V-8 engine could deliver but I admit my prime days were in my past. Oh, I remember the day PaPa brought me home. PaPa was boasting to NaNa of my make and model, being a 1960, Ford-100, 186-hp, 292-cu.in., V-8 engine. I was the fastest of my kind at that time. My special two-tone bright white and vermilion red paint job does not look that special anymore.

Though, now, a little on the faded side. Wow, has it been almost 60 years? Throughout the years, I have prided myself as being a trustworthy companion, chipped paint, clogged cylinders and all.

CHAPTER 14

Jodie

I eased out of the motel room and walked to the motel office. I had been so tired when I checked in, I remembered the clerk required me to pay in advance but I could not remember for how many nights. With the little money I had, I knew I could have only paid for a few nights. I think I had slept for two days possibly going on three. Asking about the status of my room, the motel clerk told me the room was paid to the end of the week. As I walked toward Roy I thought and questioned, "Yea! Good news. I have four days to find employment and a place to live. Am I up for the challenge?"

I greeted Roy with a hug and a smile, "Thank you Roy for getting us to a safe place." With a little tap on the steering wheel Roy gave the loudest honk he could muster and we were off to find a home and a job. As I drove around town, I began to daydream of how I met Randy. For me it was love at first sight. Being home-schooled growing up, I did not have many friends my age. There were a few younger kids in the neighborhood

I was acquainted with but we really didn't have much in common.

Basically, I did not consider dating until I arrived at college. I have a friendly nature and an outgoing attitude which made me very likeable. Immediately, I made friends with the students that were in my Ranch Management and English courses. I took part in study groups and gatherings but no serious relationships developed. With any extra time, I could be found in the library researching information I used in my personal writings. My mother always preached to me, "Jodie, a degree in Ranch Management suits you well. However, you should get a minor degree in English. No matter what happens in your life, you can always get a job with a degree in English." At the time, I didn't realize the extent of the statement, "no matter what happens in your life."

* * *

Toward the end of my second year of college, there was a tragic accident causing the death of my parents. I made myself return to school trying to fulfill my promise to my parents that I would be a college graduate. But it took every ounce within me to get myself out of bed, dress and go to class each day of my remaining college years. Those final years of college were a total blur to me. Sometimes, I try to remember my graduation ceremony, definitely a moment to be proud of, but without mom and dad to share my achievement with, my graduation came and went without notice. I remember focusing on getting to NaNa and PaPa's as fast as I could that summer of 2012.

* * *

As I was daydreaming, I recall it took some time for me to get accustomed to country life. Rising early in the morning, with the cockle-doodle-dos of the rooster, for starters was totally a new experience. Then, luckily early to bed with the setting sun was a lifesaver. My body ached from the top of my head to the bottom of my feet. But a nice soak in a tub of hot water, soft comfy bed with sheets smelling of the fresh country air and just knowing NaNa and PaPa were down the hall allowed my mind to relax into a restful night's sleep.

During those months, after arriving at NaNa and PaPa's farm, I wanted to stay busy. It helped keep my mind from dwelling over the loss of mom and dad. I did not want to accept the fact that my parents were no longer with me. I knew mom and dad had devoted their lives for my happiness and well-being. In many cases my parents deprived themselves of niceties to make sure I had all that I needed. I wish I could tell them that they were all I really needed. Making myself accept the loss of my parents fills me with unimaginable sorrow, heartache, and pain. So, for years, I have deeply denied and repressed my feelings of loss.

During that summer, I spent hours in the kitchen baking with NaNa and even more time in the barn working with PaPa. I was determined to give Roy renewed life. I could not bring my parents back but I could welcome a new friend, a 1960 Ford F-100 truck. PaPa and I cleaned the engine, changed the oil, and replaced spark plugs, lights and wiper blades. Roy received a new brake job and four new tires. The best replacement item of all, the very heart of the matter, PaPa and I installed a brand-new battery. It took a full day of washing and waxing to give Roy his deserving shine. Every minute was enjoyable for all. Before long, with a fresh tank of gas, Roy's engine was humming, ready to hit the road. PaPa and I grabbed NaNa, and the three of us jumped into the cab and off we went. To PaPa and NaNa, it felt as if they were on their first date again. I was thrilled to share such memories with them.

CHAPTER 15

Roy

Jodie and PaPa worked day and night restoring my life. With every turn of the screwdriver and twist of a lug nut, I began to come alive again. It was like it was my first birthday, although it was 2012 and I was born in 1960, but who's counting.

Jodie and PaPa gave me new tires, spark plugs, and brakes. The surprise feature was an updated radio. I was born with an AM radio. PaPa played many songs on my original radio and sang at the top of his lungs serenading NaNa back in the day. But Jodie told PaPa my new radio she installed played AM/FM radio and CDs. I was not sure what FM and CDs were but Jodie seemed thrilled about them so I was too.

NaNa sewed new covers for the seat in my cab to match my exterior, titanium white and vermilion red. But the best gift of all, a new battery, my heart. Jodie and PaPa wore themselves out with my wash and wax job but I must say, "I felt and looked brand new."

They all three loaded up and I took Jodie, PaPa and NaNa for a ride they will always remember.

CHAPTER 16

Jodie

Still lost in my daydreams, I remember fall and winter 2012 came and went like a blink of an eye. Spring 2013 appeared. PaPa and NaNa enticed me to join them going to town one Saturday afternoon. PaPa and NaNa thought it would be a nice break for all of us. PaPa and NaNa also knew there was a Rodeo performance that afternoon that they kept a secret from me. I drove Roy with his newfound look, along with NaNa and PaPa down Main Street. I was surprised to see the town decorated with rodeo banners along the street, on all the street-lights, and in shop windows. There was excitement in the air.

I parked Roy at the Rodeo Grounds, bought three tickets and PaPa, NaNa and I took our seats to watch the Grand Promenade. We all had a great time. The rodeo atmosphere was a wonderful change of scenery from the farm chores. I glanced across the arena and noticed a billboard poster showing a picture of the best looking cowboy I had ever seen. The advertisement in huge lettering stated: Special Performance Today, Randy

"RC" Cargill, World Renowned Rodeo Rider and Roping Cowboy on his sure-footed horse, Buck. The ad was intriguing. I was beyond anticipation. I couldn't wait to see Randy Cargill's performance.

And what a performance it was. After the team roping, bronc riding and barrel racing competitions, the special performance from Randy "RC" Cargill and Buck began. Randy roped objects on the ground, objects in the air, even spectators in the stands. I was thinking to myself, how fun it would be if Randy roped me. Next, Randy mounted his trusty steed and rode around and around the arena performing unimaginable stunts. The performance ended with the crowd on their feet cheering and Randy and Buck taking their bows.

I saw people forming a line beside the concession stand. I eased over to take a look and saw Randy offering autographs and Buck welcoming back rubs. I quickly got in line. When it was my turn, I realized I only had my rodeo ticket. I stuck the ticket out for Randy's signature as I met his deep brown eyes gazing into my bright blue eyes I inherited from NaNa. For me, at that moment, all time stopped!

CHAPTER 17

Roy

Jodie worked hard the moment she stepped foot on the farm. I could tell Jodie wanted her mind to get lost in her work. I guess that helped her not think about her parents, Brad and Dorothy. Then one day, surprisingly, PaPa, NaNa and Jodie jumped into my cab. Jodie steered me toward town. Driving down Main Street, there were red, white and blue banners hanging all around. NaNa said the town decorated for the rodeo. I could tell all the townspeople were excited. I was not sure about this rodeo thing but I was willing to give it a go.

I watched from the rodeo parking lot. I saw cowboys falling off of jumping animals and clowns running away from bulls. I thought those rodeo people had lost their minds. The townspeople seemed to enjoy the craziness, though. The roar of the crowd was nonstop.

CHAPTER 18

Jodie

PaPa and NaNa told me that Randy Cargill's farm was in the next county, Dandy County. They said after Randy hung up his spurs finishing his rodeo career, he started managing his family farm in Dandy County. NaNa and PaPa knew Randy's family; Sue and Tom, Randy's parents and twin brothers Pete and Sam. They said, Sue and Tom lived and worked the farm all their adult lives while raising their three sons. PaPa and NaNa told the story that Randy enjoyed country living but his brothers, Pete and Sam, not so much.

PaPa continued the story saying, when Randy was 10 years old, the Rodeo came to Dandy County. Randy was fascinated by the pure strength of the cowboys as he watched them bulldog steers and hold on for dear life for their 8 second bucking bull rides. Randy was astonished by the horses' skills and training performing extreme movements at the cowboys' commands.

Randy was hooked. From that moment on, Randy trained day and night. He taught himself to rope, practicing for hours roping every hitching post he could find. Randy learned to be competitive, he needed a trained cutting horse. He worked extra chores saving his money to purchase his hope-to-be riding partner.

A few years later, the rodeo cycled through Dandy County again. Of course, Randy and family attended every performance of the 3-day competition. At the end of the last night of the rodeo, as the spectators were leaving the arena, Randy saw a sign advertising an Appaloosa Quarter Horse named Blaze for sale. The advertisement stated Blaze was specially trained for roping. Sue and Tom knew Randy had trained and worked hard saving to purchase a horse someday. Given this opportunity, Sue and Tom helped Randy buy Blaze.

Within a few years Randy was old enough to compete. Randy and Blaze set out to compete in every rodeo they could travel to. About that time, Pete and Sam chose city life searching for their dreams. It really was no surprise, come early 2013, Sue and Tom, with mutual consent of all family members, decided to leave the farm with Randy and travel to a warmer climate and live near Pete and Sam.

* * *

As I was showing PaPa and NaNa my autographed rodeo ticket, we were surprised to be greeted by Randy "RC" Cargill. Randy introduced himself in such a way trying to find out my name and where I lived. After a few hellos, PaPa and NaNa joined the exiting crowd, leaving me to visit with Randy.

A few minutes later, I rejoined NaNa and PaPa standing next to Roy. I told them Randy asked me to come see his farm the next day. Randy gave me directions and said he looked forward to seeing me in the early afternoon.

CHAPTER 19

Roy

After the show, Jodie was super excited telling PaPa and NaNa about some guy named Randy and that she was going to drive me over to his farm the next day. Oh, my antenna went up hearing this news. Jodie seemed so electrified. I was sensing we all might short circuit.

CHAPTER 20

Jodie

Come noon the next day, I was driving Roy off on a new venture. I turned the wheel steering Roy off the main highway to travel a county road for a few miles. Then the road suddenly turned into a dead end. At first, I thought I had made a wrong turn. Then I saw a gate over on the left side sporting a huge iron symbol "RC". I told Roy, "I guess this is the right place." I drove Roy and I through the gate and traveled up the caliche road.

As Roy and I approached the top of the drive, my heart skipped a beat. There was Randy standing on the front porch, looking better than fine. He was wearing a plaid cowboy shirt, the kind with the pearl snap buttons, let's say fitted rather than tight blue jeans with a crease, black leather boots with a heel and a black Stetson hat with a braided band. Beyond looking at Randy himself, the real eye catcher was Randy's belt buckle shining brightly on his studded belt. Come to find out later, the buckle was one of the many trophy buckles Randy won in the rodeo roping competitions.

Randy helped me out of the truck. We sat on the porch visiting, sipping a glass of sweet tea. Randy asked me if I liked to ride horses. Few knew but riding horses was my favorite pastime although, I rarely had the opportunity. I responded, "Yes, I would love to ride." Randy said, "Great, I have Cream and Sugar saddled ready to go." I looked at Randy funny hearing him say Cream and Sugar. I guess Randy saw my surprised look and said, "Cream and Sugar are good spirited, easygoing mares. Come, I'll introduce you."

* * *

For a brief moment, hearing the words cream and sugar, I had a flashback to my childhood. When I was a young girl, I would crawl up on my dad's lap and he would share his breakfast with me; bacon, eggs over easy, biscuits (or sometimes toast) and cream and sugar coffee. I had a special mug with the face of a king on it. My dad would pour a little coffee in the mug and I would load the mug with cream and sugar. The best part was drinking the last sip which was mostly warm and creamy undissolved sugar.

* * *

I instantly fell in love with Cream and Sugar. The horses were beautiful showing off their white coats with a blanket of brown spots on their hips. True markings of Appaloosas. I told Randy, "It is hard to tell them apart." Randy explained the mares were sisters. Cream was just a few years older than Sugar. Randy showed me his buddy,

Buck in the barn stall. I remembered meeting Buck at the rodeo and was amazed to see how muscular he was.

Randy looked at me asking, "Are you ready for a ride?"

Am I ready for a ride?

I gave Randy a nod and mounted Cream or Sugar, I was not sure. Randy mounted up and off we went. Randy and I rode by a few pastures. He showed me his old friend, Blaze and shared his rodeo championship stories winning competitions riding Blaze. Blaze now enjoyed grazing the green pastures in retirement.

CHAPTER 21

Roy

The next day arrived and Jodie and I met this guy named Randy. My take on the guy; he looked too good to be true, dressed in a fancy shirt, jeans, boots, hat. And you talk about a showoff. Just look at that belt buckle he is wearing. It was bigger and brighter than one of my chrome headlights.

I kept a close eye as I watched Randy and Jodie visit on the porch. Then they mounted some horses I heard Jodie call Cream and Sugar and disappeared for hours. I was worried for Jodie. This guy was practically a stranger and Jodie went riding off in the country with no backup.

It was almost dark. I decided I better go find her. I popped my brake and began to roll down the hill. A horse wearing a halter with the name Blaze in shiny gold letters across the muzzle started running beside me. About that time, I saw Jodie and Randy riding up in the distance. I threw on my brakes. I didn't want Jodie to know I was "over my carburetor" concerned for her. Jodie came up to me saying, "Sorry Roy, it looks like you slid down the hill. I guess I forgot to set your brake. I will be more careful next time." That was a close call. I got away with that one.

CHAPTER 22

Jodie

Randy swept me off my feet. He surprised me with my favorite loves; chocolates, and roses of all colors. He always attached love notes to my gifts. I would find love notes tied to Cream and Sugar's manes as we saddled the horses for our daily rides.

* * *

A few months later, Randy asked me to marry him. Without hesitating, I said, "Yes!"

CHAPTER 23

Roy

This behavior continued, Jodie and I driving over to Randy's day after day. Randy showered her with candy, flowers and notes. The way Jodie smiled and turned red as she read the notes made me think Randy was trying to sweep Jodie off her feet. It worked.

* * *

I wish Jodie would have hesitated before she said, "Yes!"

CHAPTER 24

Jodie

PaPa and NaNa were thrilled for me seeing that I was so happy and in love. To them, Randy seemed to be a fine gentleman that would love and care for me. We had a small wedding inviting a few neighbors and family. Randy's parents and brothers came to the wedding, too. It was the first time I ever met them. I felt a bond immediately and was happy to have parents and siblings in my life even if they were actually considered in-laws.

CHAPTER 25

Roy

Jodie and Randy were married. Jodie and I moved to what Randy called the RC farm. Jodie seemed happy so I played along. I just wish I did not have to be parked by Randy's huge trailer pulling truck. Randy said his truck was the top of the line being a 2012 Ford F-150, 3500 hp, V-8 engine truck. It even had 6 tires, double on the rear axle. Randy called it a Dually. I called it an overrated Duly.

It took me some time to settle in, living on the RC farm. I loved when Jodie and I lived with PaPa and NaNa. But I knew I needed to keep an open mind for Jodie's sake. I watched Jodie and she seemed right at home. Jodie would tell me as we made trips to town, "Roy, I think I have finally found my home. Randy makes me very happy." With Jodie happy, I am happy and I dismissed any reservations I had.

CHAPTER 26

Jodie

Randy was still involved with the rodeo circuit with his roping exhibition performances. However, during the days he was home in between rodeo performances, Randy and I enjoyed our time together, relaxing on the farm. Sure, there were chores to handle during the week but come Sunday, I would cook a comfort meal of roast, rice and gravy for us. Randy and I would sit on the porch swing letting our lunch settle then mount up on Cream and Sugar for an afternoon ride.

During one Sunday ride, Sugar and I were galloping along when Sugar reared up. We accidentally woke a timber rattlesnake from its Sunday afternoon nap and the snake was not happy. It was an uncommon behavior but the snake came after us. Sugar was dancing around trying to get away from the rattler as it tried to strike her heels. I was holding on for my life.

Suddenly, Randy appeared with a limb he picked up out of the brush and commenced to fight off the snake. Randy was able to pin the rattler to the ground while Sugar and I made our escape. Sugar and I were so frightened, we galloped full speed back to the barn. Randy jumped on Cream and raced after us. Back at the barn, I gathered what was left of my wits but I was worried about Sugar. To calm my concerns, Randy examined Sugar for snake bites. Randy gave me a thumbs up, that Sugar was clear, no snake bites. We gave Cream and Sugar a bucket of well-deserved oats and flakes of alfalfa. Randy did not mention the fate of the snake to me and I did not ask.

CHAPTER 27

Roy

I tried to relax on Sunday afternoons. As the time rolled around, I knew Jodie and Randy would go for a horseback ride. I could see Jodie and Randy swinging on the porch then they would mosey over to the barn. Every time Jodie went riding, oil would bubble up in my engine, giving me an uneasy feeling. Even though I knew Jodie would be with Randy, I stayed on high alert until I could put my headlights on Jodie again.

One Sunday afternoon, Jodie and Sugar (or was it Cream), I could not tell them apart, came running full speed back to the barn. Usually, Jodie and Randy would ride the horses back to the barn at a slow walk. Immediately, I knew something must be wrong. Jodie's face was white as a sheet. She was trembling from hat to boot. I watched as Randy came racing to the barn. He checked the horse then took Jodie inside. I heard them talking about a snake attack. If I would have been there, I would have let that snake feel a little tire pressure. I would have shown that snake who was boss and that he better leave my Jodie alone.

CHAPTER 28

Jodie

When it came time for Randy to meet up with the Rodeo Circuit, standing by Roy, I would watch Randy as he hitched the trailer to his heavy-duty truck, loaded Buck and drove off in a different direction each trip. Randy would be gone for a month or two at a time. During those days, I worked the RC farm, doing daily chores and caring for the animals. To keep my animal husbandry skills honed from my college training, I volunteered with the local chapter of the Future Farmers of America. The FFA, as most referred to the organization, taught students to be future farmers, learning about agriculture and caring for animals; rabbits, goats, sheep, cattle, horses and many others. Several times a year, the students brought their prize animals to the stockyards for judging. I helped judge the different animal categories but, I enjoyed my time judging horses the most. I admired every horse's physique and stature, so strong, so powerful.

* * *

While Randy was away, I busied myself creating what I considered fun projects. One of my fun projects, I believe, to the neighbors' dismay, I decided to test my talents at painting. Not really knowing much about the task at hand, I went to the hardware store, purchased five, 5-gallon buckets of red paint, the biggest brush I could find and started painting the barn. I didn't realize until I got back to the farm, the shade of red paint I bought happened to be the same red color of Roy's side panels and fenders. I guess I must like that shade of red.

From the pasture, Blaze whinnied and nickered at me as I powered through the task. I suppose Blaze likes that shade of red, too. When Randy returned home, I think he thought he had turned up the wrong drive. Seeing the barn's new look, Randy didn't say much. He told me the neighbors commented the barn could be seen for miles. I accepted their comments as compliments as I contemplated my future projects.

* * *

When Randy traveled with the rodeo, I always made time to visit PaPa and NaNa several times a week and help them with their chores. When I wanted to escape all of the chores, I worked at the library. The library was quiet and peaceful reminding me of my early college years when I spent most weekends working on writing essays for the school periodicals. As I would reshelve the library books, I would tuck away in a corner and read a few chapters of the newest rom-com novels.

* * *

I knew Randy and Buck were exhausted each time they returned home. I would help Randy unload and feed Buck, giving Buck a good stack of alfalfa to munch on. Then, I would treat Randy to every cowboy's favorite meal; steak and potatoes. In the evening, Randy and I would snuggle by a campfire, eat s'mores and drink hot chocolate. I would play the guitar and sing "ole cowboy" songs. We would doze off to sleep under the stars.

CHAPTER 29

Roy

I enjoyed being with Jodie while Randy was away. It gave me great pleasure as Jodie stood by me and waved goodbye to Randy, Buck, and his fancy truck and trailer. During these times, Jodie thought of so many activities and projects for us. We would go to the stockyards on occasion. I admired Jodie as she mingled with all the different animals. The animals whether it be goats or horses seemed to be at ease around her. Jodie beamed as she put her skills into action. Everyone around just loved her!

* * *

One project Jodie dreamed up, I think, maybe, should have remained a dream. However, one day Jodie and I went to town to buy paint. She announced she decided to paint the barn. She chose vermilion red paint. I was thrilled Jodie wanted to paint the barn the same color as me. But I am not sure the neighbors felt the same. Jodie is so special.

* * *

Of course, I always enjoyed when Jodie and I went to visit PaPa and NaNa. I could hear everyone speak of the good times.

* * *

I admit when Jodie and I went to the library, I got lonely sitting in the parking lot waiting for hours. I guess it was time Jodie needed to personally recharge. As we drove home from the library, Jodie would be smiling. I knew how she felt. I felt the same way when my battery got a charge.

* * *

Randy would return, Duly, trailer and all. Jodie would jump with joy. I, not so much. My bumpers would begin to drag. Jodie would dote over Randy cooking his favorite meals, singing to him by the campfire. I could tell all of this made Jodie feel good. Me, not so much. At least they did choose to fall asleep under the stars laying in my truck bed. I kept my tailgate down so it was easy for Jodie to hop in.

CHAPTER 30

Jodie

But, as the years passed, our romance seemed to lose its' glow. When Randy returned home, he sat in his chair and drank whiskey all night. Favorite meals and campfires were of no interest to him, anymore. I finally admitted to myself that I was of no interest to him, anymore. I blamed myself for our failing marriage. I was in a standstill not knowing what to do.

* * *

There was one occasion Randy was working a rodeo event not too far from Dandy County. I thought it would be fun to join Randy and relive the first time I saw his marveling performance and possibly rekindle our relationship. I was hoping spending this time together might add the spark in our lives that we so desperately needed. There was just enough time to make the matinee performance. I grabbed a few things, jumped into the cab of my forever, devoted truck and steered Roy to join Randy at the rodeo.

I was dazzled by Randy's performance as if it was the first time seeing his amazing roping and riding skills. After the show, I was anxious to find Randy and rave about his performance. As I rounded the corner of the arena, I saw Randy being congratulated by another woman. Immediately, my inner self wanted to jump to negative conclusions. But I spoke to myself quickly and decided the woman must be one of the barrel racers that travel the same rodeo circuit, that she was just a rodeo acquaintance.

I went to approach Randy but paused for a moment and watched. Randy and the woman walked toward a nearby trailer and went in. I followed. I peeked in the window to see a bare chest and it was not the bare chest I had known for years. To my dismay and heartbreak, by watching Randy's actions, it was a bare chest he found with much delight.

I was crushed. At that instant, I died a thousand deaths. I turned to run but I stopped myself for a second. I took out my cell phone and snapped a picture. Then, I ran. When I arrived at the rodeo, thinking it was a good idea at the time, I parked Roy near Randy's truck and trailer. Not such a good idea now. I eased back around the corner, mixed in with the departing crowd and made my way back to Roy. I merged Roy into the line of trucks and trailers exiting the fairgrounds and turned toward home.

Or was that really home? Where was home?

I was able to keep my composure until I got to the interstate. Then, I began to sob. The tears flowed making it difficult to see the road. But, at that moment, I really didn't care if I met my death or not. Inside I was already dead.

CHAPTER 31

Roy

When Randy would prepare to travel for his rodeo performances, I would watch from under the tree where I was parked in the shade. Randy would hitch the trailer to the Duly, load his horse, Buck into the trailer and they would take off and be gone for some time. While Randy was gone, I would drive Jodie over to visit PaPa and NaNa. I was happy being with just PaPa, NaNa and Jodie. It was like old times.

One time when Randy was away, instead of going to visit PaPa and NaNa, Jodie says, "Roy, Randy is performing close by. Let's go surprise him and watch his matinee performance." Jodie parked me by the Duly and trailer while she watched the show. After the show, I could just see around the Duly as Jodie returned. Jodie seemed overly excited to greet Randy. But as she rounded the corner I could see and I know Jodie could see Randy was with someone else. It appeared Randy was being way too friendly with this someone else.

I saw Jodie almost buckle at her knees. My antenna went up. I knew something was wrong. Jodie disappeared for a moment and I panicked. Then she came up along my passenger side, slid into the cab then drove us weaving in and out among the exiting vehicles. I guessed she was trying to mix us in the best she could with the younger cars and trucks. Jodie was quiet for a while then she began to cry. I was very worried. I had never witnessed Jodie sobbing so deep from within, her emotions bursting out of control.

Jodie was not keeping her hands on my steering wheel. Several times I thought we were going to drive off the road and land in the ditch. I tried my best to keep it together for both us. Had Jodie given up, given up on life?

PART II

CHAPTER 32

Roy

I was excited to be driving with Jodie down the main street of Honest, Texas. Jodie said we had to find a job and a home. I guess that is what we were doing although, I could tell she was heavy in thought as she barely pressed on the accelerator. I slowly moved along also heavy in thought. I was remembering when Jodie rescued me from under the tarp. I had been driving just a few years with Brad, Jodie's father. I remember racing PaPa and NaNa to the hospital the night of Brad's birth. It seemed Brad grew up so fast. Before you knew it, Brad was old enough to drive. He would give me a tap on the hood to say good morning and off we would go returning to the farm as the sun set.

I remember watching Brad from the parking lot practicing football after school. Then, Brad and I would give Dorothy Tucker a ride home. I could tell Brad was sweet on Dorothy. Brad always had a red rose sitting on my seat for her. To help Brad make his move, I would hit a bump causing Dorothy to sit closer to Brad. Brad would put his arm around Dorothy as they eased on down the road. I could tell they were very happy. Although, I thought they both acted a little goofy. I think people call it puppy love. I am not sure what puppies had to do with it, but I knew Brad and Dorothy had it.

One day out of the blue, Brad parked me in the barn and covered me with a tarp. I thought I was going to suffocate. I held the air in my intake valve as long as I could. I could not see what was happening but I heard Brad telling everyone goodbye. Months earlier, I remembered Brad talking about college. Brad said he and Dorothy wanted to study at the same university in the east.

Oh, poor NaNa. I could hear her crying. Peeking through a hole in the tarp I could see PaPa and NaNa holding on to each other waving goodbye to Brad. I waited in the barn. I just knew PaPa would rescue me. I guess PaPa was too sad to drive with me anymore since Brad went to college. I stayed covered with that suffocating tarp for years. Brad would visit the farm during the holidays but he didn't stay long enough I guess to merit getting me out of the barn, airing up my tires and taking a spin around town.

A few years later, PaPa and NaNa said Brad and Dorothy were getting married but were not coming back to country life working on the farm. Papa said their work was better suited for living in the city since Dorothy studied Art Appreciation and English, she was able to get a job as a curator for a contemporary art museum. And because Brad studied construction design in college, he landed a design job for an up-and-coming architectural firm. I was not sure what all of that meant but I knew PaPa and NaNa were proud of Brad and Dorothy but were very sad at the same time. PaPa and NaNa missed having Brad and Dorothy closer in their lives.

* * *

One day, NaNa came running to the barn telling PaPa that Brad and Dorothy were on their way to the hospital having their first child. A little while later, NaNa came running to the barn again to tell PaPa, that Dorothy and Brad have a baby girl. NaNa said the baby's name was Josephine Dorothy Hall. I heard PaPa and NaNa talking about the baby's name. PaPa said it sure was a long name for such a small child. NaNa agreed so they called her Jodie.

Hearing all of this good news, I thought, I wish I could have been there to help them get to the hospital. I am a natural. I know the best routes and I always watch my speed.

* * *

I remember seeing Jodie for the first time. She was a young girl. I heard her brag to PaPa that she was eight years old. It was during the 1998 Kay County Fall Harvest. PaPa, Brad and Jodie wandered around the barn. PaPa showed off his woodworking and carpentry skills he used to make some shelves for NaNa to use when cooling her pies. I hoped they would walk my way. I tried to shuffle my fenders but I was very stiff having sat in one position for so long.

Every year Jodie and family would come visit and attend the Fall Harvest. Every year I tried to get their attention. The cobwebs and spiders had taken over my area of the barn. Family and friends visiting the barn could not see me. One year I heard PaPa comment that Jodie and family were coming to the Fall Harvest on their way to take Jodie to college. Wow, Jodie was already old enough to go to college. Seeing Jodie that year, I could tell she was excited. Jodie and family came the next year, too. I thought everyone looked great and seemed happy.

Then the visits stopped. I didn't know what to think. PaPa and NaNa were very upset. PaPa rarely came to the barn. Finally, Jodie came to the farm two years later. But only Jodie came. I did not know where Brad and Dorothy were. I remember seeing Jodie look at a picture of Brad, Dorothy and herself taken at the first fall fest the three shared. Jodie began to weep. Putting two and two together with my limited knowledge of the human world, I realized Brad and Dorothy were no longer with us. I felt so sad for Jodie. Now I understood why PaPa and NaNa had halted their lives these past years.

* * *

As Jodie wandered around the barn that day, I was playing the hot/cold game. She would walk close to me then get distracted and walk away. I did not want to lose my opportunity to be discovered. I shifted and shifted trying to show any part of me that I could. Finally, I wiggled the tarp off of one of my bumpers. Bingo! I heard Jodie tell PaPa, "Look what I found!" When Jodie pulled off the tarp, I leaped to the rafters and back. Before long, PaPa, NaNa and Jodie restored my insides and outsides. I was raring to hit the pavement. I remember summer 2012 was the best summer ever.

CHAPTER 33

Jodie

I suddenly came back to present day seeing a huge Help Needed sign in the window of the Honest Texas News office. I was not sure what help was needed but thinking of my experience working in the library and writing periodicals in college might get my foot in the door. I parked Roy out front and headed for the entrance. It was about 10:00 a.m. I thought the morning news chaos may be over and I could try to schedule an interview. I was concerned I did not have a résumé handy nor did I have any reference letters.

If needed, I decided I could find the local library and use their computers to generate a quick résumé. For reference letters, though, I was at a loss. Truly, the only career professional I was even remotely acquainted with was PaPa and NaNa's attorney, Mr. Riley. I visited with Mr. Riley a few times in the past helping PaPa and NaNa with a property survey of the farm they wanted to update.

Looking in Roy's rearview mirror, I realize I am not suitably dressed for seeking employment but I put my biggest smile on my face and prayed for the best. The door to the news office was an oversized, thick wooden door. I used all of my strength to pry the door open wide enough to slip in the office. I looked around at this spacious room with skyrocketing ceilings. I could see the room was actually two-story, designed so one could walk around the second floor while viewing the first floor. The railing around the upper floor was made of beautiful mahogany wooden spools. The spiral staircase leading to the second floor was made the same. There were beautiful original oil paintings up the spiral staircase. Such a unique design.

I wish Dad could see this awesome architecture and Mom would gasp eyeing these original oils.

I continued to look around. Still, no one in sight. I noticed a tall counter in the corner with a posted sign. "If you don't see me, ring bell." I wondered who "me" was. I was skeptical at first. I thought about leaving. Then, I quickly remembered I had only a few days to find a job and a home. I rang the bell!

* * *

I was surprised but nothing happened after I rang the bell. No one appeared. I rang the bell again. This time more forceful for a louder ring. Still no one. Muttering under my breath, "This is ridiculous," I started searching the office for someone, anyone. Seeing a door labeled Employees Only, I decided to take my chances. Walking through the door, I found a room of printing presses and shelves stacked with reams of paper. I heard a noise and was startled. Suddenly from behind the printing press, covered in black ink a guy pops up. I jumped back with a shriek!

An ink smudged face guy greeted me in astonishment saying, "Hello!"

Gathering myself, I gave a quick, "Hi," in reply.

"Sorry, I was not expecting anyone. The press ran out of ink on the last paper run this morning so I was trying to refill the cartridge." Looking down at himself realizing he was one big ink smear he said humorously, "Well, maybe I got some ink in the cartridge. I will know tomorrow with the morning run."

"Allow me to introduce myself, my name is Jason Ward. I am the proprietor of the Honest Texas News, he announced proudly. May I ask with whom do I have the pleasure of speaking with?"   I stammered saying, "My name is Jodie Hall." With all of the commotion, for a minute I forgot why I was there. "Oh, uh, I saw the Help Needed sign in the window. I am here to inquire about the job. Not to sound rude, but from my perspective, it seems you do need some help."

Realizing he must truly appear unsightly to his unknown guest he replied, "Touché, you are correct, Mrs., Ms. Hall?"

"Ms. Hall."

I was slightly stretching the truth. I am not officially a Ms., but I am going to make sure to become a Ms. as soon as possible.

"Well, then Ms. Hall, what newspaper skills can you contribute?" he asked. I straightened myself and with my most confident expression stated, "I have a strong background in journalism and I am well-versed on many issues. I am organized, a multitasker, and self-driven."

He responded, "Awesome, you are hired. Can you start tomorrow?" I was taken back. I never thought getting a job would be this easy.

What about a résumé, references?

I did not want to suggest any questions. Stuttering, I said, "Sure. Absolutely. Thank you, thank you very much. What time shall I be here tomorrow?"

"5:00 a.m."

When I heard 5:00 a.m. my head began to spin. I thought I best leave before he changed his mind. I bid Jason Ward farewell and found my way out as quickly as possible having to manhandle the front door the same as when I entered.

The years getting up with the roosters may payoff after all. I can do this, 5:00 a.m., no problem.

CHAPTER 34

Roy

Seeing Jodie's face coming out of the newspaper office told me something great must have happened. Jodie got in and said, "Roy, we did it. I have a job at the newspaper. I start in the morning at 5:00 a.m." Oh my, did Jodie say 5:00 a.m.? I hope we get to sleep early.

* * *

I wanted to make sure I got Jodie to her new job on time. At first, I thought it was overkill when Jodie and PaPa installed my new radio. Never thought I would use all of the features. But my radio has an alarm that is going to come in handy.

I made sure it was set to sound off before 5:00 a.m. I didn't want Jodie to be late for her first day at the newspaper.

Jodie

I kept hearing a honking noise. It got louder and louder. Suddenly, I realized it was Roy's horn. Had it short circuited? I glanced at the clock as I made my way to the door to check on Roy. In bright red numbers I read, 4:45. Oh my gosh! I can't be late for my first day of work. This Jason guy was nice to hire me but he can be nice to fire me, too.

Roy

My super radio alarm is working but I think Jodie may have slept past her alarm. I am blaring my horn now. I have to wake Jodie. Several of the motel guests opened their doors giving me their not-so-happy looks. It didn't matter. I was hoping Jodie would open her door and come check on me thinking I have a faulty horn cable. Then, I would know she was awake. This was a moment of stay hired or be fired. I had to help Jodie stay hired for the sake of both of us.

Jodie

I threw on my only other outfit and raced outside to check Roy's horn cable. With Roy's age, even though PaPa and I performed a major "Roy Restoration," some things we could fix and some things we could not fix. It seems Roy's horn sounding off anytime it wanted to was a special "Roy" feature.

CHAPTER 35

Jodie

I was pleasantly surprised. My first day of work, all seemed to fall into place. I followed Jason's lead. I learned how to load and feed the paper, make the proper cuts and folds. I even tried my hand at refilling the ink cartridges realizing getting covered in ink was inevitable.

Seeing me covered in ink this time, Jason could not hold back a belly laugh. I could not hold back either and joined in the laughter. It felt great to laugh. My spirits were lifted. Jason announced, "Looks like you could use a break. I know I can. Plus, I am starving. Want to go to the diner for the Tuesday lunch special; hamburger, fries and apple pie on the side?" I found myself enthralled with Jason's humor and demeanor. Hearing fries and apple pie, I quickly replied, "Yes!"

Walking outside, Jason was reminded his mode of travel was Eddie, a bicycle he found at the thrift shop. "I arrived in Honest, Texas via the bus line. I really didn't see the need for a car since I was spending most of my time at the newspaper. And since most destinations in Honest are within walking distance I figured the best solution was Eddie. However, today it is mighty hot to be walking." Jokingly, I think, Jason adds, "Although, Eddie does have a banana seat, we both may be able to fit on."

Quickly, before I found myself riding with Jason on the banana seat I chimed in, "I have a great truck. His name is Roy. I am happy to drive us to the diner. I can't guarantee cold air conditioning but I am sure it will be cooler than walking." Jason and I hopped in!

CHAPTER 36

Roy

I was excited to see Jodie walking over to me. Jodie was a mess. She was covered in black ink. I wondered what happened. This Jason guy was walking over to me, also. I was thankful to get a good look at him. I needed to check him out making sure he was on the up and up. To hire Jodie on the fly was unnatural. I know how special she is but, he doesn't.

CHAPTER 37

Jodie

After Jason and I ordered the Tuesday special, Jason became inquisitive asking me tons of questions inquiring of my past. At this time, especially having just met Jason, I was not prepared to go in depth nor graze the surface of the answers to questions regarding my past. Also, Jason was my boss. I quickly turned the tables saying, "You mentioned you arrived in Honest on the bus. What was that all about?" Jason turned red and shyly answered, "Well, the short of the long story is, my family has a newspaper business up north. I have worked there full-time since graduating from college. It came time to set out on my own. I hopped on the bus and headed south to start my own newspaper. As the bus entered town, I read the sign, "Honest, Texas, 2019 Population 254, Everyone Welcome!" Traveling down the main street of town I did not see a local newspaper office. So, I got off the bus, deciding to make the 2019 Population, 255." I shook my head in agreement adding, "That sign is a life changer!"

I think I would like to make the 2019 population 256! Is such an occurrence even feasible?

CHAPTER 38

Roy

I enjoyed listening to Jodie and Jason talk as we drove to the diner. Jodie played a CD in my fancy radio, a George Strait song. Jason tried to sing along with Jodie but I don't think country western music was in his wheelhouse. He told Jodie, "Iconic singers are more up my alley; Frank Sinatra, Tony Bennett, Bing Crosby. Sometimes I get a wild hair and play Elvis." Jodie laughed and smiled. I am seeing glimpses of the Jodie that found me in the barn just a few years ago. Is she finding herself once more?

CHAPTER 39

Jodie

I was spending most of my day at the newspaper office. Unfortunately, I didn't have the time I needed to look for housing. I did peruse the newspaper each day as the print was flying on the paper rolling by ream after ream, checking for any houses available for rent. Nothing. I mustered the courage to engage in a housing conversation with Jason. "I am hoping to find a house for rent. I have been watching the newspaper ads but haven't seen anything available." Jason nodded saying, "I found the same situation when I arrived in Honest. I could not find rental property. Instead, I managed to buy a duplex just a few blocks over from the newspaper office. It has proved to be a perfect location for me. The thing about it is, I only need one side, but to make the deal, I had to buy the entire house. The other side is still vacant. It has furnishings but no occupant. Want to take a look?"

What a blessing!

I could not believe what I was hearing. I excitedly yet apprehensively replied, "Sure."

"Great! I think our work is finished here for the day.

You and Roy want to follow Eddie and me and I can show you the house?" Without hesitation, Roy and I made our way to 2202 Jubilee Street.

Jubilee Street?

Following Jason and Eddie, all the streets we passed had encouraging names; Bliss Street, Delight Street…

Honest, Texas is full of surprises. I wonder what Roy and I may find at 2202 Jubilee Street?

I found the duplex very inviting. The furnishings Jason provided were warm and soothing; a fluffy blue sofa with multicolored striped pillows, a cute white table with four chairs situated in the kitchen nook. The chair cushions were covered in floral brocade material. Jason said, "The kitchen is somewhat small." With beaming eyes, I replied, "I think it is perfect." The kitchen cabinets were painted white with subtle chrome knob handles adding a slight detail. A rose patterned curtain hung in the kitchen window above the sink complimenting the chair cushion coverings. I was feeling a sense of home.

Jodie, Jodie wake-up!!! Such a home costs money of which you have none.

Coming back to reality, I looked at Jason saying, "This is a wonderful home. You have done a great job with the furnishings. It would be lovely to live here but I am not sure I can afford the rent. Speaking of money, I don't believe we have ever discussed my pay rate.

Before I get too far ahead of myself, I need to ask, what is my salary?"

I was guessing from the look on Jason's face, he had not given the matter any thought.   Noticing Jason quickly thinking off the top of his head, putting on an executive face, flips the questioning back to me, "What do you think is a fair salary for your talents?"

I thought if there ever was a time to toot my own horn, this is the time. In the back of my mind, I could hear Roy tooting his horn encouraging me. I began listing my qualities. Jason listened with respect and curiosity. "I have a college degree in Ranch Management and English. My ranch management skills you have already seen with my ability to control the printing press and ink cartridges." I paused with a smile then continued, "I do believe I can add more substance to the newspaper. Not to say that what you have isn't terrific. It is. For me, I would like to write a weekly column sharing experiences and words of encouragement to readers. I can write a sample piece for you to consider if you would like."

At first, Jason seemed speechless. Maybe all of my qualifications were too much for him. He acted like he just weathered a storm. The way Jason hesitated I wonder if he has ever hired employees before. He mentioned working at his family's newspaper business. We have been enjoying our time at the newspaper together, it really has not seemed like work at all. Maybe he feels the same way.

In an effort to regroup and save face, Jason manages, "Ok."

"Awesome, I can have the piece on your desk in the morning after we get the newspaper circulated."

Jason still regrouping says, "Ok."

After that entire discussion, there was still the salary and rent issue at hand. I was not sure of the salary amount I should request to include enough money for a monthly rent payment. So, I ask, "What is the rent amount you are asking for the duplex?" I swirl around taking in the quaint surroundings hoping he responds with a number I can afford and a salary I feel I deserve. As Jason hems and haws, I quiver for a moment thinking maybe I was too assertive.

Jason hands me a piece of paper and a pen. "Write a salary figure and a rent figure you would like." Now, I am on the spot. Well, it is now or never. I wrote two numbers on the paper and handed the paper back to Jason. Jason examining the paper asks as a way to lessen the tension in the room, "Which number is the salary number?" I immediately spouted, "The larger number." By the time I got the words out of my mouth, I saw the smile on his face. He was just teasing me. I smiled back.

Jason looking at the numbers again says, "Hum, I think we should take the larger number and triple it. Then when it comes payday, I will pay you and then subtract one-third for the rent and you keep two-thirds. That is if you would like to rent the duplex." At this moment I was so wishing I had given more effort in math class back in the day. Jason had me totally confused with his one-third, two-thirds scenarios. I tried to calculate quickly but realizing I was getting nowhere I said, "Sounds fair. Yes, I accept the salary and yes, I would like to rent the duplex."

Now, from the look on Jason's face I could tell he was relieved that all of the discussions were behind him. He responds, "Great!" However, I wanted to make sure I had the go ahead for the column. To clarify, I ask "I can write the column, yes?" "Yes, I think your column is an excellent idea. Let's run your first story Monday. Would you like me to help you move your things to the duplex?" Coming back to reality, I was embarrassed for Jason to know I only had a small duffel, a few boxes, and a backpack to move. I quickly replied, "Thank you, but I am sure Roy and I can handle it."

CHAPTER 40

Roy

Jodie has been in that house with Jason for a long time. I have tried to angle my headlights to get a better view but I was parked sideways. This Jason guy is still a stranger. I got a good vibe driving Jodie and him to the diner for lunch. I hope that vibe holds true.

CHAPTER 41

Roy

It is Monday. Jodie is excited to print her first article today. Sitting in my cab before going into work, she read the article out loud making sure there were no mistakes. Jodie is finally revealing her thoughts and feelings.

Jodie

I thought Monday would never get here. I am typesetting my first article. I pitched the name of the column to Jason, "Living Past Shadows." He said, "Run it." That is newspaper lingo, I think.

Honest News Column: Living Past Shadows

Article One

"Introduction"

The best way I know to begin is with an introduction. Hello everyone, my name is Josephine Dorothy Hall but everyone calls me Jodie. I want to thank everyone in Honest, Texas, all 254 citizens, for your warm welcome. I also want to thank one of your newest citizens, Jason Ward, the proprietor of Honest Texas News for allowing me to write a weekly newspaper column, "Living Past Shadows."

I admit I have lived the last few years of my life in denial. In fact, I truly thought to introduce myself using a ghostwriter name. Facing facts, I know that was just more denial. As of today, my life of denial ends and my forever freedom begins. I know to have something different I must do something different. Therefore, with each column posting I will face feelings of heartache, suffering, grief and pain that I have denied for years. Tragic happenings that have occurred in my life that I did not want to accept will be unveiled and reckoned with.

Through my writings it is my intent to help all that may be suffering or have suffered such pain and are living in denial face their fears, disappointments, failures and suggest ways of "Living Past Shadows" going forward in life.

CHAPTER 42

Jodie

Jason reported to me, "It looks like your column is a hit. Readers are stopping me on the street, cornering me at the diner, asking me all about you." Jason encouraged, "I think you need to keep doing what you are doing. We are putting Honest Texas News on the map."

I was thrilled. I instantly knew my next story.

CHAPTER 43

Roy

I guess it was becoming routine. Monday mornings before going into the newspaper office, Jodie would read her weekly article out loud to me. She said she wanted to make sure there were no mistakes. I know in her heart she wanted to share with me. She knows I always have her back. Companions for life.

* * *

Honest News Column: Living Past Shadows

Article Two

"My Trusty Truck"

Most people share stories of adventures they recall with their siblings, neighbors, good friends. The best adventures I recall sharing are with my trusty truck, Roy. I found Roy the summer of 2012. Having recently graduated from college, I arrived at my grandparents to begin my career as a ranch manager. My parents had died in a house fire two years earlier. They were my life and now were gone. I had no home to return to. All belongings were destroyed in the fire.

Shortly after I arrived at my grandparents' farm, I was rummaging around the barn and I see a vehicle bumper showing from under a tarp. Pulling back the tarp I revealed at the time what my grandfather informed me was a 1960 Ford F-100, 186-hp, 292-cu. in. V-8 engine. We pulled the smothered truck out of the barn into the sunlight to reveal its two-toned paint. My grandfather said originally the truck was painted with a white hood and cab and red on the sides. My grandfather announced, "Jodie, meet Roy. Roy will be your best friend for years as he has been mine and your father's."

With my grandparents' help, we restored the truck to his original glory. Roy and I have been together ever since. My local newspaper readers see Roy parked in front of the newspaper office sporting the newspaper motto, "Honest Texas News – Read the Honest Truth!"

* * *

I am the talk of the town. After Jodie posted her second article, townspeople are coming by the newspaper office nonstop showering me with gifts; flowers, cards and candy. There are also more useful items; spark plugs, quarts of oil (my favorite brand PaPa always used, Valvoline) and wiper blades. You can never have enough wiper blades.

I really think the townspeople wanted to get "Up Close and Personal" as I proudly touted the Honest Texas News motto on my bumpers and tailgate!

CHAPTER 44

Jodie

Jason calls my articles, self-help storytelling articles. I think he likes my writings. I wonder if he likes me? Or is he really all business and just likes my writings? Sometimes, I see him daydreaming. I wonder if he is thinking of me. Jodie you are kidding yourself. Most likely, he is thinking of the next day newspaper publication. Why would you think he is daydreaming of you? I can't seem to help myself but I have caught myself daydreaming about Jason. I then quickly remind myself, Jason is my boss, end of subject.

One day, Jason asked if he could drive Roy to the next town to pick up paper and ink supplies. Jason said the inventory was low and the manufacturer informed him their delivery trucks were being repaired delaying deliveries a couple of weeks. The only people that have ever driven Roy are PaPa, my dad and I. I am sure Jason is a good driver however, I have only seen him ride his bicycle. I have not actually seen him drive. I took a glance out the window at Roy and said, "I am sure Roy would love to escort you to buy supplies." Then, as a concerned mother, I added, "What time do you expect to return?"

CHAPTER 45

Roy

I wanted to show Jason what I was made of; tough steel frame, thick rubber tires and an engine that won't quit, I hoped. Driving down the road, Jason was talking to himself. He reminded me of PaPa. PaPa got a lot of problems solved talking to himself as he drove me down the road. From listening to Jason, he had a problem to solve. Should he or should he not ask Jodie to dinner. What? Oh, no! Another relationship. Jodie has not healed from the last one, her only one.

CHAPTER 46

Jodie

Jason asked me if I would like come to his house for dinner, Friday night, 7:00 p.m. I wanted to accept but I knew I best decline. But then I thought yes, it is only dinner. No, it is better to say no. I basically had a fifteen second mental tug of war then blurted out, "Yes!" All seemed feasible, I told myself. On Saturdays, we only print an evening edition of The Honest News thus eliminating a 5:00 a.m. Saturday morning wake-up alarm.

I wanted to get something new to wear. During my lunch break, I drove Roy to the women's boutique shop on Main Street. In my haste escaping Randy, I thought I remembered stashing some of my library earnings in Roy's glove box. As I rummaged in the glove box, way in the back, I saw a large envelope I had not noticed before. I recognized PaPa's handwriting.

What could this be?

I didn't have time to investigate the envelope. I only had forty-five minutes left of my lunch break. I found the small white envelope with my library money in it. I hoped I had enough money to purchase a new dress, and possibly a pair of shoes. I haven't received my first paycheck, yet from working at the newspaper. My past and present wardrobe consisted of pants and shirts that were most practical then, for working the farm and most practical now, when spilling ink while I am refilling the cartridges.

CHAPTER 47

Roy

Oh my! Jodie is so focused on preparing for her dinner date with Jason, she forgot about finding PaPa's envelope. She needs to open the envelope!

CHAPTER 48

Jodie

Friday after work, I jumped into Roy's cab and sped home. I was going to dinner at Jason's house, next door. It appeared silly, but Jason insisted on picking me up at 7:00, even though to pick me up meant he was just walking next door.

I definitely wanted to be ready when he arrived. Not necessarily ready and waiting, just ready, not late. I had cleaned the house the night before. I wanted everything to look perfect when he came in. I was thankful for the furnishings Jason had adorned the house with. I did have one special piece to add to the home decor. To take to college, my mom gave me a Vincent Van Gogh lithograph, *Starry, Starry Night*, my favorite artist and work of art. Since the tragic house fire, this was my only keepsake I had from my mother. I treasured the artwork, dearly.

CHAPTER 49

Roy

I was trying to watch through the picture window to see how dinner was going but Jason closed the shades. I don't know about this guy. Watching him knock on her door to pick her up only to walk next door for their dinner date caused me to chuckle. But I guess that was the gentleman thing to do.

* * *

Jodie got into my cab following the Monday morning routine, reading her article to me out loud, making sure there were no mistakes. I found it odd Jodie has not murmured one word about her Friday night date with Jason. I don't know what to think. It turned into a long evening. I dosed off for a while but woke as Jason walked Jodie back home. Thank goodness!

* * *

Listening to Jodie's weekly article it seems her mind is solely on work. This is a good thing. With each article I feel her wounds are beginning to heal.

Honest News Column: Living Past Shadows

Article Three

"My Role Model"

Have you ever known a person that was almost beyond approach because they were so intelligent and talented? But because of these special gifts, you were drawn toward them, mesmerized if you will that they could accomplish tasks that you would never dream of tackling. This is the way I felt of my mother, Dorothy. My mother was well respected in the national art community. She had a knack for placing artwork on display that even impressed the artist. But the day I was born my mother walked away from that life so I could have the best life she could give me. My mother tucked away all of her career dreams and ambitions to be "My Mother."

From as early as I can remember, my mother put her efforts into teaching me all she knew, including her art appreciation knowledge. When I was old enough to sit without falling over, my mother showed me posters of famous paintings and artist. She would recite out loud the name of the painting and artist. To this day, I am an encyclopedia when it comes to renown art masters and their works.

For years my mother was my homeschool teacher. There was no subject my mother couldn't master: mathematics, science, history. My mother would say, "Jodie, bring on the calculus problem. I can calculate the answer." And she did!

My mother and father were taken from this world when I was twenty years old. I feel guilty for my mother spending the beautiful years of her life teaching and caring for me. She gave up her life for me. I now reckon that she freely chose to walk away from her career. Being with me was the most important and most fulfilling part of her life. My mother loved me that deeply.

I cannot bring my mother back to this earth but I can honor her by sharing the knowledge she gave me with others. Honest Texas News readers, anytime you need help with a writing assignment at school, a math problem you cannot solve, a science experiment that flops, I encourage you to let me know. We can join forces and work together as my mother taught me to do.

My Role Model. Mom, I miss you!

CHAPTER 50

Jodie

I have to keep my mind on my work. However, I want to keep reliving Friday night, my dinner with Jason. Am I even emotionally strong enough, must less physically, and mentally prepared for another relationship? Now? But I really like Jason. I feel at ease around him, at work and outside of work. Jason makes me laugh, not that he is that funny. It is his mannerisms, his chivalry, his humility. Like his insistence picking me up for our dinner date although we were just walking 10 steps from my door to his door. How fun was that. Way cool! I felt special, important.

Jason seemed to appreciate my appearance. He complimented me on my dress, matching shoes, my earrings and my hairstyle. My earrings were a high school graduation gift from my dad. My dad told me he thought the small gold loops fit the size of my face and the embedded amethyst gems are my birthstone. For my date with Jason, I pulled my hair up in a ponytail. It had been since my young girl years that I wore a ponytail. Seeing myself in the mirror that night with my ponytail look and birthstone earrings brought back memories of sharing special moments with my dad.

CHAPTER 51

Roy

These Monday mornings with Jodie make me happy and sad. I am happy Jodie is allowing herself to mourn and heal. As Jodie sits in my cab, I try to give her protection and comfort wrapped in NaNa's upholstery covering my seat as she reads her articles out loud. But it is so painful to listen as she reads and sobs.

Honest News Column: Living Past Shadows

Article Four

"My Savior"

I confess, in this earthly world, I don't profess to be overly religious. However, in my spiritual world, I do believe in one supreme being, God. In my spiritual life, I know He is always with me and watches over me on earth. My father, Brad Hall, my earthly savior always watched over me until he and my mother were killed in a very tragic accident. The accident happened in 2010 while I was away at college. Until now, I have not shared my loss with anyone except my beloved grandparents, who too have gone to their resting place.

Recently, I found a photo of my parents and I on vacation at a nearby lake when I was a young girl. I had just graduated from Swim Lesson 101 and I was excited to try my new found skills not realizing swimming in a lake is far different than swimming in a backyard pool. I ventured out, swimming along enjoying the cool, refreshing water with not a care in the world. It seemed like hours had gone by but looking back I am sure only minutes had passed and I found myself getting tired. I turned to swim back to shore but grew more tired with every stroke. I remember thinking and praying to God, "Well, I guess this is it. God, my arms and legs are exhausted. I can't seem to move them anymore. My life has been short, but fulfilling. Thank you, God, for everything."

I took what I thought to be my last breath and began to sink. Little did I know I was closer to shore than I realized. At that time of my life, I always wore my long hair pulled up in a ponytail. Thank goodness. Within a brief moment of spiraling downwards, suddenly I was moving upwards using no will of my own. My father had been watching me all along. He sensed I may be having troubles and waded out into the lake and pulled me above the water by my ponytail.

My dad may no longer be on this earth to physically save me. But Dad, just the thought of you saves me in so many ways every day.

My Savior. Dad, I miss you!

CHAPTER 52

Jodie

think Jason enjoyed our date. At the office, he keeps looking at me while I am working. Jason's obvious stares definitely make it that much harder to concentrate. My heart wants to tell him I had a wonderful evening but my mind and emotions tell me to hold back. I will stay busy and put my attentions toward writing my next article for the column.

As I was loading the paper prepping for the evening run, Jason, I thought came over to help me. Instead, he began verbalizing a dissertation asking me out for another Friday night date.

"I had a terrific time Friday night. I hope you did as well. I was thinking it would be fun to make every Friday night a date night! This Friday night, what about a movie and an ice cream afterwards? The local movie theater, The Majestic, shows classic movies and iconic movie stars. I know you like country western music so maybe you like western movies? The Friday night feature is *The Cowboys* with John Wayne."

I was about to respond when Jason added, "Can we drive Roy, Eddie doesn't care for westerns?"

There is that humor that takes me over the top. In fact, I was so engaged listening to Jason, I accidentally weaved the paper over the top of the press instead of underneath. Paper was flying everywhere.

"Turn off the printing press power switch."

I ran to the opposite end of the printing press and flipped the switch. The press motor slowed and paper floated down from the air covering the floor. I looked at Jason. He was wearing the largest grin I have ever seen. We both broke into laugher, rolling on the floor covering each other with paper.

"Oh, by the way, you are in luck. Roy and I love John Wayne movies. We love ice cream even more. What time should we be ready Friday night?"

"The movie starts at 7:00. We don't want to miss the previews. I will come to your door at 6:30."

"We will be ready!"

CHAPTER 53

Roy

Jodie says, "Roy, Jason asked me to the movies Friday night. Would you be so kind to drive us?" With a honk, I say, "Yes!" Jodie is all smiles. Wow, two Friday nights in a row. Jodie and Jason going out together. Are they a couple now? Should I be excited or worried?

CHAPTER 54

Jodie

It was hard to keep my mind on work. I couldn't wait for Friday night. Another date with Jason. My mind was still recounting every minute of my first Friday night date with Jason. One day I found myself standing in the newspaper supply room forgetting what I had come to get.

Jason asked me to the picture show, to see a John Wayne movie. Jason said he thought I may like a western movie since I like country western music. He is so thoughtful. Truthfully, it doesn't matter to me what movie is showing. I know I will enjoy sitting next to Jason, sharing popcorn and a soda. Since we are seeing a western though, I want to dress the part. I will wear jeans, boots, white shirt and a kerchief.

CHAPTER 55

Roy

Driving Jodie and Jason to the movies and for ice cream reminded me of driving Jodie, PaPa and NaNa for a Saturday night outing. Those were great times!

* * *

This Monday morning Jodie reads me a story about NaNa. NaNa was always there for Jodie especially after Dorothy went to heaven. I know Jodie misses NaNa terribly as I watch the tears streaming down her cheeks.

Honest News Column: Living Past Shadows

Article Four

"My Heroine"

It is interesting when an object, a smell, a taste takes you back in time. I was window shopping and saw some material, yellow cotton fabric with white polka-dots. Staring at the material, in my mind's eye I could see NaNa sitting at her sewing machine. NaNa could make her sewing machine hum as she created one-of-a-kind garments. NaNa used a special stitch as her signature.

Sewing was not a skill of mine but NaNa was the greatest. I would watch her for hours sewing for friends and customers. She would let me help prep by pinning the material right sides together.

I walked in from the barn one day to find a blouse hanging in the sewing room with my name on it, signed Love, NaNa. The blouse was made of yellow cotton so it would be cool and decorative with white polka-dots. NaNa had made it special for me to wear to the rodeo that was coming to town at that time. It was spring 2013.

NaNa, you always had that unique way of making me feel exceptional. You left this world so sudden. I have been lost without you. It has been painful not to be with you, to sew with you, bake with you. I yearn to be close to you.

I found a sewing machine at the thrift store. I was not able to replicate the beautiful blouse you sewed for me but I found some yellow and white polka-dot material and made a kerchief in your honor.

My Heroine. NaNa, I miss you!

CHAPTER 56

Jodie

I could feel myself falling head over heels for Jason. I memorized every detail about him. His dazzling hazel eyes, his huge smile. His wavy brown hair and his very manicured mustache. When Jason kissed me, my entire body tingled, from his mustache tickling my lips to my toes twitching in my boots.

As Roy and I were taking a casual drive I imagined my life with Jason. I knew I would feel loved, safe, respected, and appreciated. I could never imagine Jason causing me disappointment. Jason was perfect! With the windows rolled down, I started yelling at the top of my lungs for the world to hear, "I love Jason."

CHAPTER 57

Roy

After my drive with Jodie the other day, I am here to declare, it is official, "Jodie loves Jason." Yikes! I think Jodie is moving way too fast. I need to throw on the brakes.

* * *

Honest News Column: Living Past Shadows

Article Five

"My Everything"

I tend to put people on pedestals. These people don't know I have raised them high above everyone else to some degree thinking they are immortal. Then, I am awaked by the fact they are truly mortal and mortals make mistakes. Sometimes these mistakes are deliberate but most times the mistakes don't intend to hurt others but do. The point is these people never asked to be placed on this "Jodie" pedestal. It was all my doing. Most of the time they fall from the pedestal never knowing I had raised them up there above others because I loved them so dearly and thought the world of them.

PaPa, my grandfather deserved to be raised up on the "Jodie" pedestal. He never faltered and fell. He was my knight in shining armor. When I needed a shoulder to cry on, PaPa was there. When I needed work to take my mind off of sad things, PaPa was there. When I needed protection, PaPa was there. PaPa had the magic touch. He always knew when to show up, what to say, what not to say. And his smile was infectious, yet warm and comforting.

PaPa loved like no other. I call it unconditional love. He loved NaNa that way and I know he loved me that way. Because I was, he loved me. I didn't have to win the gold medal or make an A+ on my assignment to be worthy of his love. He loved me how I was, any time, any day, no matter what.

When he looked at me and smiled, no words needed to be exchanged. I would look back at him and I could hear, "Jodie, I love you."

PaPa, I look into the heavens each day. I can see you smiling at me and I hear, "Jodie, I love you."

My Everything. PaPa, I love you, too.

CHAPTER 58

Jodie

I admit I was consumed with the joy of love. My days were happy, my nights were happy. I felt my life had meaning. All things were falling into place. Then I got a shot of reality. I was still married. I had never filed for divorce. Fearing repercussions from Randy, I delayed preparing divorce papers. My feelings for Jason gave me hope for a happy future. I told myself I was strong enough to end the past allowing a brighter future to come.

I suppose I was secretly hoping Randy had moved on and would not be hostile accepting this marriage finality. I decided to contact Mr. Riley asking him to prepare the divorce papers and send them to Randy. I specifically asked Mr. Riley not to divulge my address in Honest, Texas, just in case. The last thing I wanted was for Randy to ever show up in Honest.

CHAPTER 59

Roy

Jason asked Jodie if he could drive me to the city. He was meeting with an advertising firm. Jodie was fine letting Jason and I go to the city on business. She knew I would keep Jason safe. In the meantime, Jodie said she had her eye on some boxes filled with magazines that needed filing. She said she would be busy the rest of the day.

* * *

Jason and I were off to the big city. His meeting did not last long. I was glad so we could get back to Jodie. Then Jason said he had an errand to run. Jason parked me in front of a jewelry store.

Oh, no! Is Jason carrying a little black box?

CHAPTER 60

Jodie

While Jason and Roy were spending the day in the city, I was glad to have time to myself at the newspaper office. As I worked, I was dancing and singing with George Strait, *If You Ain't Lovin' (You Ain't Livin')*. I was happy because I knew I was lovin'.

Toward the end of the day, I neared the bottom of the stack of magazines I was filing. I liked to keep magazines organized and easily accessible. The magazines made great reference material for my column articles. As I thumbed through the few remaining magazines, I thought I glimpsed a photo of Jason. Quickly, I went back through the stack. There was Jason, in living color on the cover of Forbes magazine, with that forever loving smile of his.

What?

The headline read: **Jason Ward, son of Jeffrey Ward – Ward Enterprises, New York, New York, Inherits Billion Dollar Empire.**

What?

I didn't know whether to be happy or sad. Be happy, Jason a billionaire or sad reckoning with the fact Jason had deceived me. Arriving in Honest, Texas on a bus. Cycling on Eddie every day to work. I don't think that is the way billionaires travel. Trembling, sobbing I fell into the chair, wiping tears from my eyes, trying to read as the magazine article relayed the truth.

CHAPTER 61

Roy

I was happy to be back to the newspaper office to see Jodie. I guess she heard Jason and I coming up the street. Jodie was outside waiting for us, with open arms?

I don't think so. Jodie seems upset. She is waving some papers in the air with fury on her face. Jason saw Jodie's demeanor and took a hard swallow. He said, "Well Roy, I knew it would come out sooner or later. I was just hoping it would be later." He sadly placed the little black box in my glove box and went to face the music.

Wait, wait. Jason knew what would come out? I thought Jodie had found her Happy Ever After. But, maybe not?

CHAPTER 62

Jodie

Jason tried to plead his case but at the same time he did not understand why I was so upset with him. "Why didn't you tell me you are a billionaire, that your family is upper echelon? The article said you graduated with a Master of Business degree from Harvard! You must have had a big laugh as I am telling you of my degree in Ranch Management. I need to leave. Goodbye!"

CHAPTER 63

Roy

Jodie's eyes were red and puffy when she got into my cab. Jodie cried, "Roy, will I ever learn? Why do I time after time put them on that pedestal? Why do I think more of them than is really there? I know they are going to go plummeting down." She sobbed, "Why do I want more for them than they want for themselves?" Hanging her head, she wept sobbing, "I feel so foolish. No more. I quit."

Then, I saw the magazine cover laying on my seat. Jason a billionaire?

CHAPTER 64

Jodie

I was pulling together the few things I had added to the duplex making it my home, I thought. I decided it best to pack and take Roy on down the road not looking back, again.

I thought Honest, Texas was my forever home with my forever love. I guess not. I suppose it has just been a dream.

CHAPTER 65

Roy

I can see Jodie packing. Oh, I wish she would wait. I see Jason knocking at her door but she is not letting him in. Oh, I wish she would.

CHAPTER 66

Jodie

I heard another knock at the door.

I wish Jason would go away. It is over.

The knocking persisted. I finally decided to give in and open the door. I immediately tried to slam the door and lock it but Randy, got his boot in the doorway and pushed himself in. In his typical rage, Randy was waving papers in my face. I held my ground. He started to come after me. I quickly showed the picture of his trailer escapade. Randy was taken off guard. He stepped back. I ordered, "You sign those papers and get out of here. Never come back or I will show the world their famous rodeo star has fallen from his mighty steed. Those rodeo belt buckles of yours will shine no more."

Randy knew I meant what I said. He signed the papers, threw them on the floor and started out the door. Jason must have heard our loud voices from next door and came to check on me. Randy, Jason and I stopped in our tracks as the love triangle manifested itself. Randy looks at me. I look at Jason. Jason looks back at me, then at Randy.

I was wishing Roy's supposedly short-circuiting horn would sound off about now causing a distraction and it did. All three of us looked over at Roy. Roy's lights started flashing. Roy was now the center of attention, not me.

I had no intention of introducing Randy to Jason or vice versa. I gave Randy the "leave now and never come back" stare. Randy jumped in the Dually, burned some rubber and drove away.

CHAPTER 67

Roy

Randy finding us in Honest, Texas caught me off guard. When I saw Randy, Jason and Jodie squaring off, I knew I had to do something. That horn trick always works. I threw in the light show for good measure.

I could tell when Randy and the Duly drove off they were never coming back. I don't know what Jodie used to send him on his way forever. But it looks like it worked. I know what I have always wanted to do. Take all of those belt buckles and stuff them in the Duly's exhaust pipes.

I am thankful Randy, Duly, belt buckles and all are gone. I know Jodie is thankful, too.

So why is she still packing?

CHAPTER 68

Jodie

I retreated inside to recover. Jason followed me. I catch my breath and bear my heart to Jason.

"The first day I met you I was not completely truthful. I was a Mrs. trying to become a Ms. When I arrived in Honest, Texas, I was running, running from many things. I was running for my life and from my life. I was trying to escape a life of denial, loneliness, feelings of abandonment and heartbreak. As you have read my articles in the newspaper column, I am sure you have figured out the denial, loneliness and abandonment but you did not know about the heartbreak. For five years, I thought Randy, my husband loved me as I had loved him. Or I wanted to believe he loved me. I held on, staying in the marriage for years not to admit failure. Once PaPa and NaNa passed away, there was nowhere to hide, no protection. So, I ran, I ran fast, never looking back. Then, I met you!"

CHAPTER 69

Roy

Jason sat in my cab totally confused trying to sort things out saying, "Roy, I love her. It is a shock to find out there was a husband. But I am happy for Jodie that guy is gone. I hope she can be happy for herself."

Jason continued, "Looking back I should have told Jodie about my family. I was so taken with Jodie, her beauty, her smile, her laugh. She can do anything and everything. I love Jodie. I want to spend the rest of my life with her. I forgive her, will she forgive me?"

Get the ring out of my glove box and tell her now!

* * *

Jodie put all of our things in my truck bed and crawled into my cab. She said, "Roy, I need to post my last article." And she began to read out loud, shedding years of anguish, devastation, loss, and rejection with each tear.

Honest News Column

"Living Past Shadows"

Accepting a failed relationship is the first step to healing, to "Living Past Shadows" allowing yourself to go forward. I am taking that first step. I am accepting that I had a failed relationship. I loved a man with all my heart, with all of my soul. I thought he loved me in the same way. Time told the truth. It seems he loved the thought of me. He loved that I looked good by his side. He loved that I was intelligent, I could figure things out on my own. He loved that I could run the ranch in his absence.

Unfortunately, all these qualities I had that he seemed to love became qualities he hated. It became a competition. He had to prove his dominance over me time after time. He was verbally abusive if I suggested an idea that could prove better than his. Before long, I had no voice, no say about any situation. I learned to keep my mouth closed or ...

There was a point in the relationship when I became aware of his infidelities. I am ashamed of myself. I tucked my tail and closed my eyes to the ugliness. For years, I have asked myself why did I stay, why did I stay in a hostile, unloving relationship. I can now answer the "why" question. I did not want to admit my relationship was a failure. I did not want to admit that the man I loved did not love me.

I did leave the relationship, but the failure came with me. That failure has kept me locked in a room with open doors. The thought of entering into a relationship again was too much to fathom, mentally, physically, emotionally and spiritually. Until now. Now I know I must move forward. My parents and grandparents that have gone before me would truly want me to be happy. I feel their spiritual encouragement to move forward. I have to forgive myself and let it go. I deserve to be happy. I want to be happy.

Coming full circle, looking in the mirror, I admit I am not the girl I used to be. I have lost a great deal, my parents, my grandparents and my marriage. Facing my losses, my sadness and my failures opens the path for me to move forward. I have a new love in my life and I don't want to waste a moment longer "Living Past Shadows" when I can be "Living Past Shadows" which I am determined to do. Today, as I close this column posting, I vow to go forward, to follow my dreams, to embrace my forever love I hope is waiting just for me.

Jason, please forgive me. I love you.

CHAPTER 70

Jodie

If I would have looked in the rearview mirror, I would have seen Jason pedaling Eddie as fast as he could. Jason must have parked Eddie on the backside of the newspaper office watching me go in to make my final article posting. I guess Jason read my article on his phone because he surprised me as I walked out of the newspaper office. We looked at each other and in unison said, "Please forgive me. I love you." We kissed and embraced never intending to let go. Jason, got down on one knee, showing me a little black box and asked, "Jodie Hall, will you be my wife forever?" Without hesitation, I said, "Yes, forever!"

EPILOGUE

Roy

Jodie and Jason are a beautiful couple. At Christmas, Jodie pulled herself into my cab saying, "Roy, we need to make sure you have a tune-up. Any day now, Jason and I are depending on you to drive us to the hospital. Honest, Texas 2019 Population is changing to 257."

When the time came, I was more than ready. I had been practicing the route to the hospital. The roads were icy this time of year. Jason made sure my tires were not squishy. Not long after we arrived at the hospital, Jason came out to check on me. Like PaPa, Jason forgot to park me in the lot. Jason says, "Roy, thank you for getting us to the hospital, safely. We were depending on you." Jason continued, "Roy, we are proud parents of a beautiful baby boy. His name is Jonathon."

I was overwhelmed. My battery overflowed with love.

EPILOGUE

Jodie

know Jonathon's favorite night-night is here somewhere as I rummage through Roy's cab. "Roy, I want to thank you for helping us bring little Jonathon into the world. You are always there for me, for us. I am looking for Jonathon's night-night. Have you seen it?"

Roy honks his horn.

"In the glove box? I will check and see."

Rummaging through the glove box, I don't find Jonathon's night-night but I do find PaPa's papers. "Roy, look what I found again, PaPa's papers. I never opened the envelope. I guess this is a good time. Let's see what the papers say. Oh, Roy, you are not going to believe this. PaPa and NaNa left us an inheritance. It is very valuable. Wow!"

As I read the papers briefly, PaPa and NaNa had asked Mr. Riley to sell the farm and belongings upon their deaths and setup an inheritance for me and my descendants. Now, I understand why Mr. Riley seemed confused when I asked him to prepare divorce papers, not estate holding distributions.

"Roy, these papers have been in your safe keeping. I think it is the best idea to let you continue to watch over this envelope. When Jonathon is old enough, honk your horn and help him find his inheritance. Until then, it will be our secret. Roy, I love you, forever."

Yea, I found Jonathon's night-night. Jason and Jonathon will be thrilled. I know this is the beginning of many wonderful nights.

"Goodnight, Roy!"

Saying goodnight to Roy, I hurry back to our duplex made into our "one-plex," our home, as Roy flashes his lights saying goodnight, I love you, in return.

ACKNOWLEDGMENTS

My devoted spouse always cheering me on and especially for his hands on skills and encyclopedia knowledge of vehicles. What a lifesaver.

My sons, family and friends for being my "critique group" and for your everlasting love, support and encouragement.

My newest friend and awesome graphic designer. Thank you, Gaby.

ABOUT THE AUTHOR

Renee Goodwin is an award-winning author of GG Life Lesson Storybook Series ® books. Renee has an undying passion for education which began at an early age. Through the years Renee has become an accomplished teacher, engineer, businesswoman, author and artist.

Renee is the recipient of the 2021 Texas A&M University Aggie Women Legacy award. She continues her legacy with her GG Life Lesson Storybook Series® books on exhibit at the Cushing Library at Texas A&M University.

Renee created her own publishing company, Goodwin Global Publishing, LLC offering authors professional contract publishing services producing quality products while establishing loyal and long-term relationships.

Renee offers GG Life Lesson Storybook Series® books and her novels for purchase on her website, personally autographed and mailed to you.

Renee is happy to announce her recent novel, LIVING PAST SHADOWS. You can read more about Renee, her children's books and novels, LIVING PAST SHADOWS, and A LOVE, A LIFE, FORGONE on her author page on Goodwin Global Publishing website.